First published in Great Britain in 2018 by Pat-a-Cake
This edition published 2019
Copyright © Hodder & Stoughton Limited 2018. All rights reserved
Pat-a-Cake is a registered trade mark of Hodder & Stoughton Limited
ISBN: 978 1 52638 273 3 • 10 9 8 7 6 5 4 3 2 1
Pat-a-Cake, an imprint of Hachette Children's Group,
Part of Hodder & Stoughton Limited
Carmelite House, 50 Victoria Embankment, London EC4Y 0DZ
An Hachette UK Company
www.hachette.co.uk • www.hachettechildrens.co.uk
Printed in China

My Very First Story Time

The Gingerbread Man

Retold by Ronne Randall

Illustrated by Susan Batori

gingerbread
man

Mum

cat

Molly

dog

cow

pony

fox

bread

jam

One day Molly and her mum decided to make a gingerbread man for their tea.

SUGAR

Molly gave the gingerbread man bright eyes and a cheeky smile made of icing. Mum gave him a sailor suit.

What a jolly gingerbread man he was!

"We can eat the gingerbread man for our tea," said Mum.

"Oh, no, you won't!" said the cheeky gingerbread man, springing up off the tray.

He jumped off the table, then ran across the kitchen floor . . . and straight out of the door!

Molly and Mum were amazed.

Quick as they could, Mum and Molly and the dog and the cat ran after the gingerbread man.

"Stop!" they shouted.

But the gingerbread man did not stop. He just ran faster, singing, "Run, run, as fast as you can. You can't catch me, I'm the gingerbread man!"

They came to a field where a spotty cow was cheerfully chomping grass.

"Stop, stop!" mooed the cow as the gingerbread man ran past.

But the gingerbread man did not stop. He just ran faster, singing, "Run, run, as fast as you can. You can't catch me, I'm the gingerbread man!"

The cow ran off after the gingerbread man. And Mum and Molly and the dog and the cat ran after the cow.

But none of them could catch the gingerbread man!

An old, grey pony was grazing nearby. When he saw
the gingerbread man, he whinnied, "Hey! Stop!"

But the gingerbread man did not stop. He just ran faster, singing, "Run, run, as fast as you can. You can't catch me, I'm the gingerbread man!"

The pony flicked his tail and galloped after the gingerbread man. And the cow, Mum, Molly, the dog and the cat ran after the pony.

But none of them could catch the gingerbread man!

The gingerbread man came to a rushing river.

"Oh!" he said. "I can't swim! How will I get across?"

A sly fox sidled up to the gingerbread man. "Why don't you hop on my back? I will help you across the river." he said.

So the fox set off across the river, with the gingerbread man sitting on his back.

"Oh, dear!" said the fox. "The water is getting deeper. You'd better hop onto my head."

So the gingerbread man hopped up onto the fox's head.

But then . . . the fox's mouth went snap, snap, snap! And his sharp teeth went crunch, crunch, munch! And that was the end of the gingerbread man.

So the cow, the pony, the cat, the dog, Molly and Mum all had bread and jam for tea that day!

Make your own gingerbread man with this recipe!

350g plain flour, 100g butter, 2 teaspoons ground ginger, 1 teaspoon ground cinnamon, 1 teaspoon bicarbonate of soda, 175g light brown soft sugar, 4 tablespoons golden syrup, 1 large egg.

1. Preheat the oven to 180°C / Gas 4.

2. Chop the butter into small pieces and add to a bowl with the flour, ginger, cinnamon and bicarbonate of soda and mix until crumbly. Add the sugar, syrup and egg, mix until it forms a firm dough.

3. Dust the surface and a rolling pin with flour. Roll out the dough to about 5mm thick.

4. Now, cut out your gingerbread people.

5. Put the shapes on greaseproof paper on a baking tray.

6. Bake until golden, about 12 minutes. If using a fan oven, about 10 minutes.

Ask a grown up to help you!

Can you spot five differences between these two pictures?